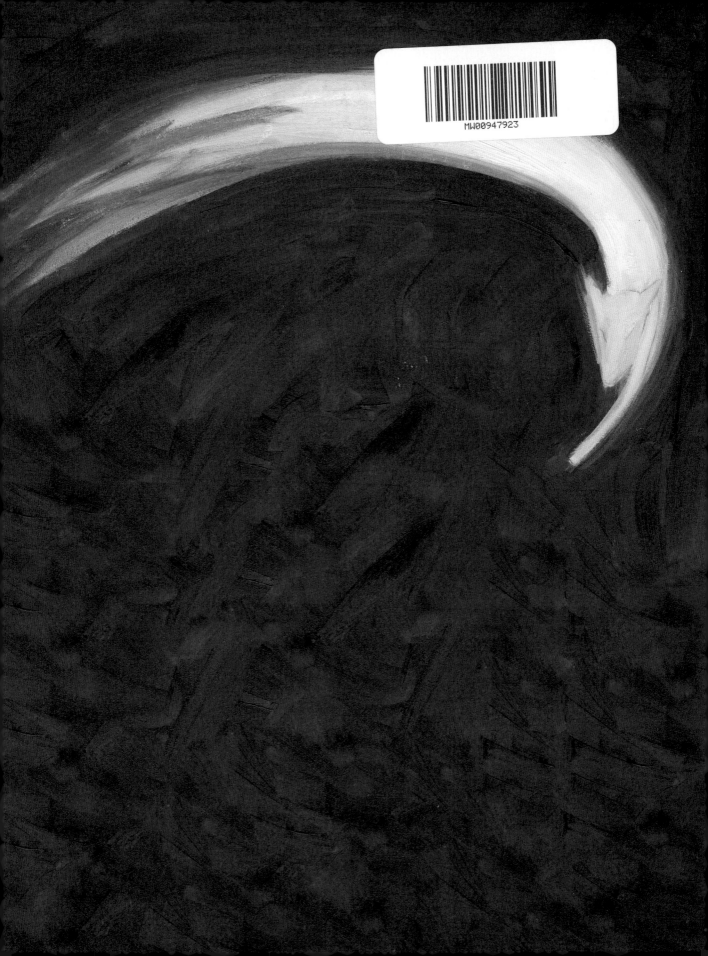

This book is dedicated to our husbands, Guy Bate and Tom Jacob;
our two other sisters, Jocelyn Canals and Jean Maltese;
our parents, Thomas and Arlene McGuire;
mothers-in-law, Adele Bate and Carol Jacob;
our fathers-in-law, Thomas Bate and Thomas C. Jacob;
and for all children who may feel different on the outside
but have beautiful inner souls.

www.mascotbooks.com

Turquoise Tail

©2018 Rachel Bate. All Rights Reserved. No part of this publication may be reproduced, stored in a retrieval system or transmitted in any form by any means electronic, mechanical, or photocopying, recording or otherwise without the permission of the author.

For more information, please contact:
Mascot Books
620 Herndon Parkway, Suite 320
Herndon, VA 20170
info@mascotbooks.com

Library of Congress Control Number: 2018907332

CPSIA Code: PRT0918A
ISBN-13: 978-1-68401-988-5

Printed in the United States

TURQUOISE

Believe in yourself! ♡ Rachel Bate

TAIL

By Rachel Bate

Illustrated by Rebecca Jacob

In the soft gentle evening, a coyote pup was born
with a *turquoise* tail to her parents forlorn.

"What is wrong with our strange little pup?
With her *turquoise* tail that stands straight up?"

Her siblings giggled as they observed her tail.
Cielo quickly skirted away, to no one's avail.

Chewing and chewing her bright *turquoise* tail,
"Please come off now!" she hysterically wailed.

"Oh dear, my tears are *turquoise* too!"
As Leroy Lizard said, "Me oh my, what's wrong with you?"

"You're a freak of nature, and oh what a sight!
You sure do stick out on this bright desert night!"

Cielo whimpered, "Please little lizard, leave me alone,
for as it is now, I do not have a home."

Word quickly spread with the desert critters of the night
of the *turquoise* tail and Cielo's unlikely plight.

"Hey sisssssss, do me a favor," Raul Rattlesnake hissed.
"Hide that tail before I add you to my hors d'oeuvres list!"

Rubina Roadrunner skimmed across the desert brush, spotting the tail she commanded, "Hush!

"Look at that hideous pup with that *turquoise* tail! My poor old eyes are sore, I'm ready to bail."

Now Cielo was devastated, her heart so distressed.
What she would do now was anyone's guess!

She silently laid her weary head upon a small rock,
while animal after animal continued to mock.

The plight of her tail no one could know,
how much it affected her beautiful soul.

Suddenly streaming across the night sky
appeared a comet where Cielo decided to lie!

A magnificent creature descended from the light.
Cielo glanced up, her eyes full of fright.

Why it was Bliss, the white coyote, with a gentle wide smile.
"Now Cielo, my gorgeous wee *turquoise* child!"

"Your beauty from within shall not go unnoticed.
You are special my friend, so please stay focused.

For what I shall tell you is excellent advice,
do not focus on hurtful words that are not nice.

For those who make fun of the way you look
are downright despicable in my big black book."

Bliss took down notes of those who are treated this way
so he could intervene and help them to not sway.

"For with your unique tail, we shall paint the desert sky
in preparation for the balloon fiesta that is hovering nearby!"

As daylight dwindled near in the New Mexico sky,
balloons gently lifted, spectacular to the eye.

For a small coyote pup with a beautiful
      turquoise tail painted the sky with Bliss.
It was a sight no one could miss!

So always think wisely before you attempt to speak.
Practice prudence, especially for those who are meek.

Paz, love, and always be a good friend,
like Bliss to Cielo, whose heart he did mend.

About the Author

Rachel Bate has lived in New Mexico for the past twenty-five years, where she has been captivated by the natural beauty and the critters that appear in her stories. She has been an elementary and special education teacher since 1985. She is passionate about teaching and inspiring her students to always treat others as they would like to be treated.

Turquoise Tail is Rachel's second children's book featuring characters who are critters of the New Mexico landscape. Just like her first book *Desert Bliss*, Rachel wrote this story in the hopes of encouraging children to follow their dreams and be mindful of others' feelings. She collaborated with her sister (and the illustrator!) Rebecca Jacob on both *Turquoise Tail* and *Desert Bliss* to create engaging, colorful pictures that coincide beautifully with the stories.

About the Illustrator

Rebecca Jacob graduated from Moore College of Art and Design in Philadelphia. In addition to Moore, Rebecca studied at the School of the Visual Arts, NYC; The Art Students League of New York; the Cleveland Art Museum; and the Pennsylvania Academy of the Fine Arts.

Rebecca worked as a storyboard illustrator and designer in New York City, Cleveland, and Philadelphia for several years prior to focusing on her fine art. She currently resides outside Philadelphia, in between travels to family in Boston, Texas, and New Mexico.